To ....

For being good.

MERRY CHRISTMAS!

From Santa

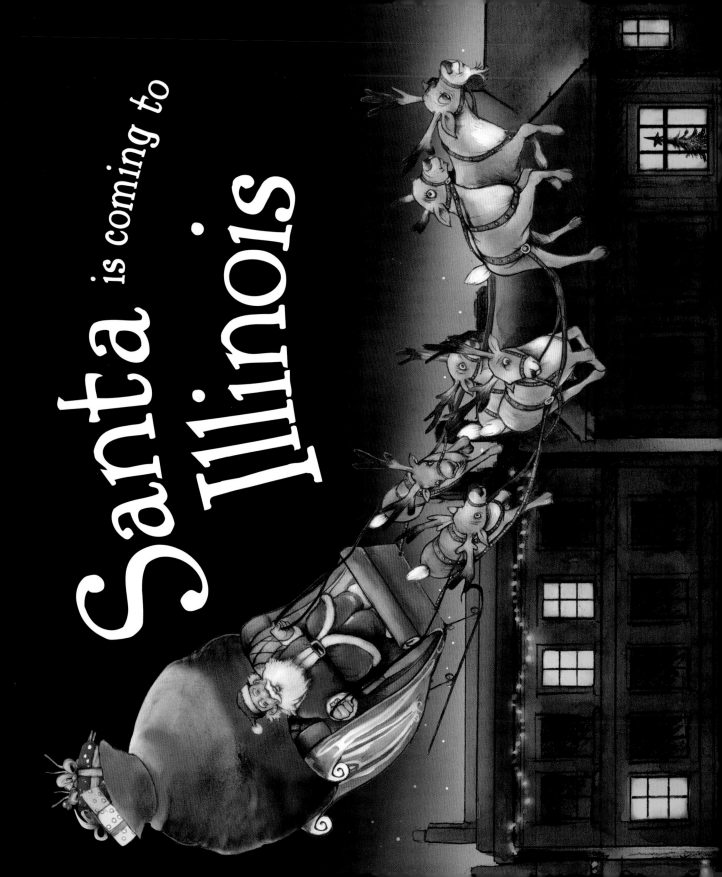

Santa *is coming to* Illinois

Written by Steve Smallman
Illustrated by Robert Dunn and Amerigo Pinelli
Designed by Sarah Allen

Copyright © Hometown World Ltd. 2013

Published by Sourcebooks Jabberwocky, an imprint of Sourcebooks, Inc.
P.O. Box 4410, Naperville, Illinois 60567-4410
(630) 961-3900
Fax: (630) 961-2168
www.jabberwockykids.com

Library of Congress Cataloging-in-Publication data is on file with the publisher.

Source of Production: Leo Paper Products, Guangdong Province, China
Date of Production: April 2014
Run Number: HTW_PO170314
Printed and bound in China
LEO 10 9 8 7 6 5 4 3 2

Santa is coming to Illinois

Written by Steve Smallman

Illustrated by Robert Dunn and Amerigo Pinelli

sourcebooks
jabberwocky

"Well?"

boomed Santa. "Have all the children from **Illinois** been good this year?"

"Well...uh...mostly," answered the little old elf, as he bustled across the busy workshop to Santa's desk.

Santa peered down at the elf from behind the tall, teetering piles of letters that the children of Illinois had sent him.

"Mostly?" asked Santa, looking over the top of his glasses.

"Yes...but they've all been **especially** good in the last few days!" said the elf.

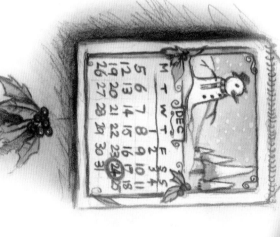

"Jolly good!" chuckled Santa,
"Then we'd better get their presents loaded up!"

Even though the sack of presents was

really, really big

and the elves were **really, really small,**

they seemed to have no trouble loading it onto Santa's sleigh. Though how they managed to fit such a big sack onto one little sleigh even they didn't know. But somehow they did.

"Splendid!" boomed Santa. "We're ready to go!"

"Er..not quite, Santa," said the little old elf. "One of our reindeer is missing!"

"Missing?"

Which reindeer is missing?" asked Santa.

"The youngest one, Santa," said the elf. "It's his first flight tonight. I've called him and called him, but..."

Just then, a young reindeer strolled up, munching on a large carrot.

"Where have you been?"

asked Santa.

But the youngest reindeer was crunching so loudly that it was no wonder he hadn't heard the little old elf calling.

"Oh well, never mind," said Santa, giving the reindeer a little wink. He took out his Santa-nav and tapped in the coordinates for Illinois. **"This will guide us to Illinois in no time."**

Crunch!

Crunch!

Crunch!

With a flick of the reins and a jerk of the harness, off they went, racing through the sky.

"Ho, ho, ho!"
laughed Santa.

"We'll soon have these presents delivered to the Land of Lincoln!"

Santa's sleigh flew through the starry night, in the wintry air, crossing over Canada. On they flew, heading south across the Arctic Ocean. The youngest reindeer was flying across Lake Superior. In the wink of an eye, the sleigh was very excited. He had never been away from the North Pole before.

They had just crossed Lake Michigan
when, suddenly, they ran into a blizzard.
Snowflakes whirled around the sleigh.

They couldn't see a thing!

The youngest reindeer was getting a bit worried,
but Santa didn't seem concerned.

"In two miles... "

said the Santa-nav in a bossy lady's voice,

"...keep left at the next star."

"But, ma'am," Santa blustered, "I can't see any stars in all this snow!"

Soon they were

hopelessly lost!

Then, through the howling blizzard, the youngest reindeer heard a faint, ringing sound.

Ding-dong!

He looked over at the old reindeer with the red nose. But he had his head down.

(Red nose...I wonder who that could be?)

Ding-dong!
Ding-dong!

Ding-dong!
Ding-dong!

Ding-dong! Ding-dong!

There was that sound again, like church bells ringing. The youngest reindeer turned around to look at Santa. But Santa wasn't listening. He seemed to be arguing with a little box with buttons on it.

With a flick of the harness and a jerk of the reins, the youngest reindeer gave a sharp *tug* and headed off toward the sound of the bells, pulling Santa and his sleigh behind him!

"Whoa!"

cried Santa, pulling his hat straight. "What's going on?" Then, to his surprise, he heard the ringing sound.

"Well done, young reindeer!" he shouted cheerfully. "It must be the Thomas Rees Memorial Carillon in Springfield. Don't worry, children. Santa is coming!"

Then, suddenly...

CRUNCH!

The sleigh hit something as it plummeted through the snow clouds.
"you have arrived!" said the Santa-nav unhelpfully.

Finally, when the snow had died down and the clouds parted, Santa discovered exactly where they were...

...stuck, right at the very top of the Old State Capitol building!

"Everybody, PULL!"

The reindeer *pulled* with all their might until, at last, with a screeching noise, the sleigh scraped clear of the Old State Capitol, and Santa steered them safely above downtown, over Robin Roberts Stadium, past Illinois State Fairgrounds, and down into Carpenter Park.

Luckily, there
was no real
damage done, but
the packages had all
been jumbled up. Santa
quickly sorted out the
presents into order again.

"All right," said Santa. "Thanks
to this young reindeer I know where
we are now. Don't worry, children,

Santa is coming!"

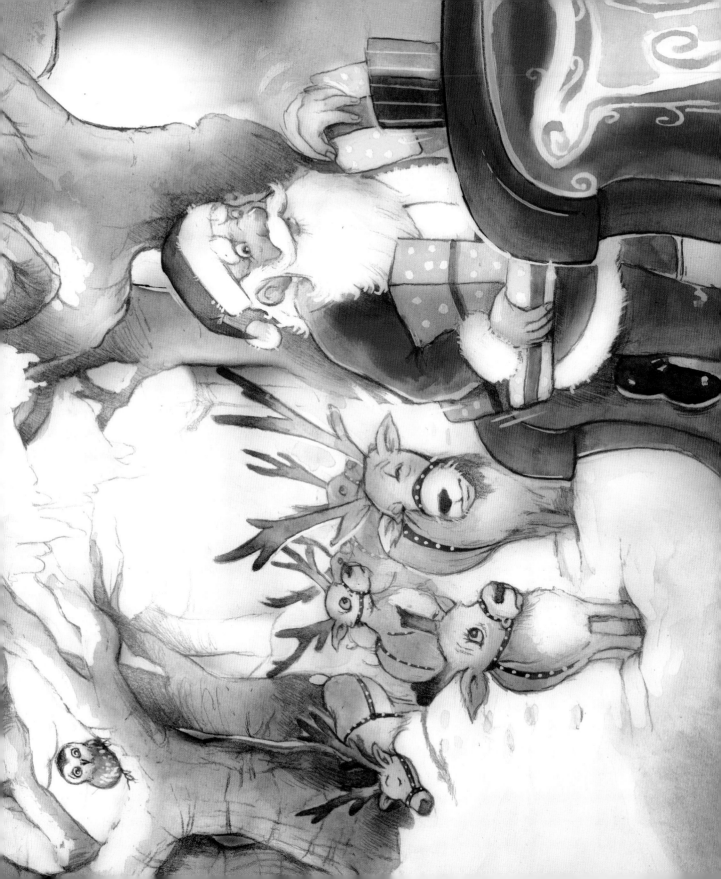

Santa drove his sleigh expertly from rooftop to rooftop all over Illinois, popping in and out of chimneys as fast as he could go.

(Which was pretty fast for a chubby fellow!)

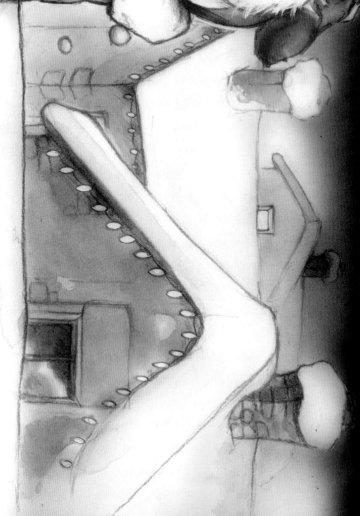

There were big chimneys in Chicago, and small chimneys in Rockford. He squeezed down thin chimneys in Peoria and plummeted down fat chimneys in Elgin.

The youngest reindeer was amazed at how quickly they went. Santa never seemed to get tired at all! And it looked like the children in Illinois were going to be very lucky this year! But the youngest reindeer was starting to feel a bit weary and quite hungry too!

In house after house, Santa delved inside his sack for packages of every shape and size.

He piled them under the Christmas trees and carefully filled up the stockings with surprises.

Santa took a little bite out of each cookie, a tiny sip of milk, wiped his beard, and popped the carrots into his sack.

In house after house, the good children of Illinois had left out a large plate of cookies, a small glass of milk, and a big, crunchy carrot.

From Champaign to Carbondale, from Belleville to Bloomington, from DeKalb to Decatur, from Woodstock to Winnetka, and ALL the places in between, Santa and his sleigh visited every house in Illinois.

Santa delivered presents to Andrew, Alison, Anna, Arabella, Archie, Ashley...the list went on and on! ...Zac, Zara, Zeb, Zoe, Zybil.

(Zybil? That must be a spelling mistake, surely!)

Finally, Santa had delivered the last present on his long Illinois list.

"Great moons and stars!" sighed Santa. "It's past midnight and my sack seems as heavy as ever! I hope I haven't forgotten anyone."

Santa opened his sack to check...but it was full of juicy, crunchy carrots!

Santa divided the carrots among all the reindeer.

"Well done!" he said, patting the youngest reindeer gently on the nose.

But the youngest reindeer didn't hear him..he was too busy munching!

Then it was time to set off for home. Santa reset his Santa-nav once more to the North Pole, and soon they were speeding above Carlyle Reservoir, over the Abraham Lincoln Library, along Route 66, and past Joliet through the crisp starry night.